Chief of the Fire Brigade

by Jay Dale

t

a Capstone company — publishers for children

Engage Literacy is published in the UK by Raintree.
Raintree is an imprint of Capstone Global Library Limited, a company incorporated in England and Wales
having its registered office at 264 Banbury Road, Oxford, OX2 7DY – Registered company number: 6695582

www.raintree.co.uk

Editorial credits
Marissa Kirkman, editor; Charmaine Whitman, designer; Katy LaVigne, production specialist

10 9 8 7 6 5 4 3 2 1
Printed and bound in China.

Chief of the Fire Brigade

ISBN: 978 1 4747 3909 2

Contents

Chapter 1 Just too busy 4

Chapter 2 Where's mum? 10

Chapter 3 A surprise 14

Chapter 4 A special guest 18

Chapter 5 Feeling proud 22

Chapter 1
Just too busy

"Sorry, Aimee," said Mum, sadly.
"I'm just too busy!"

Aimee had heard these words
many times before.
Mum was **always** too busy.
She was always too busy to watch
Aimee's football matches.
She was always too busy to watch
her dance shows, too.

"I'm **so** sorry," said Mum as she grabbed
her yellow coat and helmet from the hook.
"Dad will have to take you to football practice
this afternoon.
I have to be at the fire station in ten minutes
for a meeting."

Aimee's mum was the chief of the fire brigade.
She was an amazing woman.
Aimee was very proud of her, but ...
she was always too busy to watch
Aimee do anything!
Every day Aimee's mum had meetings
to go to.
Often at night, she and her team
were called out to fight a fire.

Dad smiled at Aimee.
Then he gently took her hand
and gave it a little squeeze.
"Come on my sunshine girl," he said.
"We'd better get going or we'll be late
for football practice."

Chapter 2
Where's mum?

After football, Dad and Aimee cooked dinner.
"Where's Mum?" asked Aimee,
as she peeled the potatoes.

"She's been called out to a fire," replied Dad.
"There was a large fire in an old building
just around the corner from the hospital."

"Oh, no!" cried Aimee.
"Was anyone hurt?"

"No," said Dad.
"It was really lucky that your mum
and her team got there so fast.
They put out the fire very quickly."

Later that night, as Aimee lay asleep
in her bed, Mum sneaked into her room.
She was covered in ash and soot,
and her hair lay flat on her head
from her helmet.

Mum leaned over and kissed Aimee gently
on the top of her head.
"Sleep well, my little sunshine girl,"
she whispered.

Chapter 3
A surprise

The next day, Aimee was late for school. Mum had been talking on her phone to the newspaper about last night's fire and had forgotten the time.

When Aimee arrived at school,
the children were sitting at their desks.
"Sorry I'm late, Mr Scott," said Aimee.
Mr Scott just smiled as Aimee
sat down next to her best friend, Gill.

"Hey, Aimee," whispered Gill.
"Mr Scott said there is a surprise
for us after break time."

"Really?" said Aimee.
"What is it?"

"Well," said Gill,
"Mr Scott said he couldn't tell us much.
He just said that there was
a very important person coming
to speak to all the children at school."

Chapter 4
A special guest

After break time, Aimee's class followed
Mr Scott into the school gym.
All the other children were there, too.
The younger children sat at the front.
The older children and their teachers
sat at the back of the gym.
Aimee sat in the middle of the group,
right next to Gill.

"Good morning everyone," said Mrs Letts,
the head teacher.

"I'd like you to all listen carefully.
Today we have a very special guest
coming to talk to us.
This person is amazing!
She is one of the bravest people I know.
While we are all safe and sound
tucked up in our beds, this special woman
and her team are keeping us safe."

Aimee's mum walked through the door
and into the gym.
She looked straight at Aimee.
She gave her a special wave
and a big happy smile.
Aimee felt so proud that the very special guest
was her mum.

Chapter 5
Feeling proud

After the talk was over, Mr Scott asked Aimee's mum if the class could look at the red fire engine.

"Of course!" smiled Mum.
"I can show the children how everything works."

Mum showed the children the different parts
of the fire engine.
She also showed them the large hoses
that went around and around.
Some children were allowed to climb
up the ladder.
Some were even allowed to sit
in the front seat next to Aimee's mum.

At last when it was time for Mum
to go, Aimee gave her a big hug.
"I'm so proud of you, Mum,"
she said.
"You are very special and you make
me feel very special, too."